CIARA and RUSSELL WILSON

With JaNay Brown-Wood

WHY Not YOU?

Illustrated by

Jessica Gibson

Random House 🏠 New York

Copyright © 2022 by Ciara Wilson and Russell Wilson
Jacket art and interior illustrations by Jessica Gibson

All rights reserved. Published in the United States by Random House Children's Books,
a division of Penguin Random House LLC, New York.

Random House and the colophon are registered trademarks of Penguin Random House LLC.

Visit us on the Web! rhcbooks.com

Educators and librarians, for a variety of teaching tools, visit us at RHTeachersLibrarians.com

Library of Congress Cataloging-in-Publication Data is available upon request.
ISBN 978-0-593-37440-5 (trade) | ISBN 978-0-593-37441-2 (lib. bdg.) | ISBN 978-0-593-37442-9 (ebook)

The artist used a combination of Procreate and Photoshop to create the illustrations for this book.
The text of this book is set in 18-point Brandon Grotesque Regular.
Book design by Nicole de las Heras

MANUFACTURED IN CHINA
10 9 8 7 6 5 4 3 2 1
First Edition

To our parents, who inspired us to live with a Why Not You attitude.
And to our children, who we are blessed to share it with.
—Ciara & Russell

To my parents, Marci and Lee, who taught me to believe in myself.
And to my husband, Catrayel, and my daughter, Vivian, who push me to be better every day.
I am because of you.
—JaNay

To my amazing family, especially you, Mom.
You always supported me throughout my creative journey
and encouraged me to follow my dreams.
—Jessica

Is there something that you dream of?
Something that you'd be or do?
Something that would make you happy
and make all your dreams come true?

Maybe you cannot stop thinking about a job you could pursue:

like an athlete, author, singer,
or the captain of a crew.

Do you find yourself daydreaming
of what you are meant to do?

Or perhaps you worry whether
your dreams are too big for you?

Take a pause, a breath, a moment.
Use your brilliance as your cue.
And then think about this question:

Why not you?

Why not you? Why not you?
You're a winner! You're so strong!

You are perfect and important—
you and all your gifts belong.

Why not you? Why not you?
You're a star! You have no fear!

You are such an inspiration.
We are grateful that you're here.

Ever heard "The sky's the limit"?
Well, that simply is not true.

Go beyond it! Keep on pushing!
You can break *that* ceiling, too.

You are stronger than you realize.
Wiser, smarter, braver, too.

There is absolutely nothing
that you can't try or reach or do.

Life is filled with many lessons.
Obstacles may block your view.
Disappointing situations
may make triumph hard for you.

Don't you worry! Keep on trying!

Soon you'll make your big debut.

It will take determination—
persevere and you'll get through.

What's your story? What's your mission?
What will you become or do?

Now's your time! The whole world's waiting!
All our hearts are set on you.

Why not you? Why not you?

You are great! You have the stuff!

You can drop your doubts and worries.
You're perfection. You're enough.

Why not you? Why not you?
You're a hero! You're the best!

Listen closely and believe it,
then let go of all the rest.

Hear these words and really listen.
Every one of them is true.
Look inside yourself and know it:
You are magic, through and through.

There is truly no endeavor
that's too hard or big to do.
Your potential has no boundaries!
You can do it—

WHY NOT YOU?

AUTHORS' NOTE

"Why not you?"

That was a sentiment we heard from our parents and families growing up. For as long as we can remember, we were encouraged to dream big and were told that the only thing standing in the way of achieving our goals was how hard we were willing to work and how much we believed in ourselves. We learned that it wasn't about being tall enough to become a Super Bowl–winning quarterback or having enough training to be a Grammy-winning entertainer—it's that everything is possible if you work hard and believe. We strive to instill this in our own children every day. It is also why we started our Why Not You Foundation, to empower the youth to lead with a Why Not You attitude. And we wrote *Why Not You?* to reach as many young dreamers as possible, and to reach those who have been afraid to dream. We want to inspire you to dream big so you can go however far you want to go and become whatever you want to be. WHY NOT YOU?